CELINE'S SALON

THE ANTHOLOGY

~Volume 2~

Edited by
Lucy Tertia George

Wordville

© 2022 Wordville
ISBN: 978-1-7391030-2-6

First edition
All rights reserved

The rights of each of the authors in this anthology to be identified as the author of this work have been asserted by them in accordance with the Copyright, Designs &
Patents Act 1988.

This book may not be reproduced or transmitted in any form or by any means without the written permission of Wordville.

Proofread by Ruby Gawe

Wordville
www.wordville.net
info@wordville.net

INTRODUCTION

Celine's Salon has built a loyal following in the theatres, pubs, hotels, clubs and (even) hair salons where the show has performed in Soho since its inception in 2016.

Celine's Salon – The Anthology Volume 1 was a labour of love, and we were encouraged by all the support and great feedback we got from that first collection of poetry, song writing and short stories. It was pretty clear that we were going to create a follow up book.

After lockdown took Celine's troop online, everyone was itching to 'get out there'. Once the gates of London were opened it seemed only fitting to take to the road for the first official Celine's Salon UK Tour.
Celine has always enjoyed gathering the widest group of writers and poets to join the monthly events, providing a platform for writers to share their work. Now the Salon was eager to hear from people further afield. Inspired by a writer's retreat in Roald Dahl's old holiday home in Tenby and a visit to Tenby Museum, Celine felt it was the Celtic voices that were calling out to join in next.

So, the circus became a travelling circus, with writers from London joining our beloved host Celine as she travelled to Derry in Northern Ireland, Glasgow in Scotland and back to Tenby in Wales.

Motivated by the quality of talent in each of these locations—established performers and first timers—it seemed only fitting that Volume 2 of our Anthology should focus on bringing together writers from the Celtic Kingdoms.

The authentic Scottish, Irish and Welsh voices inspired us with how they used language to engage the audience, to make us laugh like drains, surprise and sometimes enrage us with the wide range of subject matter and clear sense of place in their work.

Not everyone who performed is featured in this book—space wouldn't allow that, I'm afraid. But here's a collection that we think represents the talent and emotional integrity of what Celine's Salon discovered on its journey across three countries.

Thanks to all who have supported Celine's Salon in London and on the road. Do keep coming to the live events and, in the meantime, sit back and enjoy the printed version of the show.

Welcome to **Celine's Salon – The Anthology Volume 2.**

Wordville

ABOUT CELINE HISPICHE

Celine Hispiche is a London-based writer and performer whose monthly show on Totally Wired Radio celebrates diverse writing and performance. She spent three years in New York, performing stand-up comedy, returning to the UK to develop a variety of musicals and productions, performing at events and festivals around the country and across the world. Celine devised Celine's Salon to create a platform that nurtures new and established artists and offers the audience an entertaining and enlightening experience.

Thanks to all the writers, poets, singers, artists, comedians, storytellers, magicians, raconteurs and musicians who joined Celine's Salon's tour in 2022:

From GLASGOW

Ashley Chapman, Willy Copeland, Jo D'arc, Katharine Macfarlane, Maria Beadell, Thomas McColl, Mark McGhee, Lesley O'Brien, Pinky, Frank Rafferty and Keith Warwick.

From DERRY

Ritchie Beacham-Patterson, Birdwoman, Mel Bradley, Valerie Bryce, PBJ, Paul Campbell, Ronan Carr, Peter E Davidson, Joanna Fegan, Scarlett Fever, Keiran Goddard, Michael Groce, Fintan Harvey, George Houston, Hutch, James King & Ann McKay, Violet Malice, Darren McCay, Abby Oliveira, Niall O'Mianain, Frank Rafferty, Mockingbird Theatre, Juanita Rea, Lee Ann Toland, Douglas Graham Wilson and Michael Wilson

From TENBY

Meredydd Barker, Nerys Beattie, The Curious Florist, Shirley Hammond-Williams, Siobhan Lancaster, Ros Moore, Heather Moulson, Kevin O'Dowd, Billy Parker, Bob Reeves, Emily Vanderploeg and Susie Wild.

CONTENTS

Curtain Raiser

1. Celine Hispiche 3

Part One: Glasgow

1. Lesley O'Brien..9
2. Jo D'arc 11
3. Frank Rafferty...15
4. Thomas McColl..17
5. Ashley Chapman...21
6. Katharine Macfarlane 23
7. Pinky...29
8. Maria Beadell...30
9. Mark McGhee...32

Part Two: Derry

10. Frank Rafferty 37
11. Michael Groce 40
12. Mel Bradley..42
13. Valerie Bryce 44
14. Keiran Goddard...47
15. Ronan Carr...48
16. PBJ...51
17. Niall O'Mianain..54
18. Juanita Rea..57
19. George Houston..59
20. James King & Ann McKay............................62

Part Three: Tenby

21.	Ros Moore	66
22.	Celine Hispiche	71
23.	Susie Wild	74
24.	Heather Moulson	78
25.	Kevin O'Dowd	81
26.	Billy Parker	82
27.	Anonymous	86
28.	Siobhan Lancaster	87
29.	Nerys Beattie	90
30.	Bob Reeves	94

CURTAIN

Acknowledgements 98

CURTAIN RAISER

Celine Hispiche

CELINE HISPICHE

THE SKYLINE BALLET

Cranes like elegant monsters
Perform the skyline ballet
New wave metropolis going up
Georgian buildings crumbling down

Goodbye Astoria and the Greek fish and chip shop
Dingy alleyways where naughty things go on
Girls in neon fishnets
Walk in marshmallow high heels
Fuelled by vodka red bulls

Modern day gin lane
At St Giles Circus
Entices the goths and punks to its wares
Rowdy bawdy electric music fills the air

Tarts and the arts congregate
Creating a living breathing canvas
Projectile splatters
Rain pitter patters
Like a Dickens illustrated plate

New wave old wave
Acid house culture wave
Hip hop bee bop

The carousel of contemporary
Takes you on a swirly whirly ride

The modern-day Hogarth
Puffs on his rollie
And soaks up images
In his twinkly eyes

A cloud of ostrich feathers
Encases the beautiful babe
Hob nob vintage boots
Pinstripe dapper
With pencil moustache
He's having a giraffe

Alienesque burlesque
What's next?
High kick
Military robots
On checkered tiles
Where's David Lynch when you need him?

Diary of a word eater
Falls in love with a panel beater
Licking the kerbs of Charing Cross Road
Belgium waffler, eighties back comb

Hip hop
Bebop
Hot scotch
Top notch

Fly the fashionistas
Pouring out of clubs
Sequin capes, mango vapes
Disperse into the night

Uber is the boober
No bolts to whisk away
Burping workers
Suburban night crawlers

Modern Lego
Architectural blow
Cherry lights
Skim the air

Bring on the cranes
Take off the clowns
A rapture of bows
To the skyline ballet

Tip Top
Loud Pop
Bravo the Skyline Ballet!

Céline's Salon Glasgow

PART ONE

Lesley O'Brien
Jo D'arc
Frank Rafferty
Thomas McColl
Ashley Chapman
Katherine Macfarlane
Pinky
Maria Beadell
Mark McGhee

LESLEY O'BRIEN

CARBETH

Velvet green steppin stanes fir fairy feet
that flee o'er the lull o the uisge beatha
it's ma kirk ah must come wance pur week

She hauds me a baby o the universe
nestlin against her weary breast
o bracken, birch an elm

She disnae scold me but she wins me o'er
wi whispers o contentment
fae the bow o her Campsie helm

She blaws nae wind
but ah feel the cauld kiss o winter
oan ma cheek, her gentle reminder that
aye ye must come wance pur week.

DUMGOYNE GODDESS

By Dumgoyne mound there's a goddess tae be found
by day she lies a mummy in her tomb
at night she rises oot o Dumgoyne's womb

Wi bramble coat an fern fat fleece
she stumbles doon by roots an clabber
midst stoor an beast an glowerin moon
she sups Craigallan watter

By swirlin crow she dips her toe
an floats upon a lily pad
west highland walkers come an go
oblivious tae this bonnie lass

But Carbeth Hutters know her ways
an feast upon her halcyon days
but if ye truly wish tae meet an touch her heart
by Froggy Lane alone at dusk ye start.

INTAE THE NIGHT SHE DANCES

Intae the night she dances, she dances
swaying with the branches she dances, she dances
on tippy toes she dances, she dances
skin, moon-milk as she dances, she dances
laughs, grasps for the moon as she dances, she dances
stepping over stones she dances, she dances
skipping and a hopping she dances, she dances
by willow and oak she dances, she dances
hair, swaying, swirling she dances, she dances
hands on hips she dances, she dances
by rowan and birch she dances, she dances
arms swaying with the branches she dances, she dances
intae the night she dances, she dances
intae the night she dances, she dances
intae the night she dances, she dances
intae the night she dances, she dances

Lesley O'Brien is a singer, storyteller and poet and has worked for Glasgow Women's Aid for almost 30 years.

JO D'ARC

COAL DUST

From coal dust my heart is made
From coal dust my bodies baked
From coal dust my thoughts unfold
Feel coal dust in every pore

---

see my wings reflecting gold
they grip the sunshine
avoid the cold
recognise my brothers' mold
the place i should stand
the place i fold
it's hard to shift a mind that's old
ancient feelings
broken souls
where i learned to be so bold
to take a beating on a grassy knoll

From coal dust my heart is made
From coal dust my bodies bake
From coal dust my thoughts unfold
Feel coal dust in every pore

---

sit under table steal a beer
i hear debate of angry fear
i understand how we're treated here
bullied bashed
while we bristle and seer
energy of people proud
fueled by illustration that they hear our sound
broken spirits gritted teeth
passion peaked in a poignant speech

From coal dust my heart is made
From coal dust my bodies bakes
From coal dust my thoughts unfold
Feel coal dust in every pore

---

more than just a memory
a wider connection lives in me
hack back through the moving seeds
hands black with silt hearts beating to be free
strong and fearful
wrong and right
moving in time with an invisible light
a broken spirit builds our soul
ignite a people
no limits hold

From coal dust my heart is made
From coal dust my bodies bake
From coal dust my thoughts unfold
Feel coal dust in every pore

           I s - cream in-side
            I s - cream in-side
             I s - cream in-side
              I s - cream in-side
                I scream
                  I scr
                  ea
                  m

FOREVER LOVERS

You shouldn't expect people to change
Said Jim. 43. Divorced
That was the problem with her you see
She tried to control me
She tried to make me what she wanted me to be
But I want to be me
You see
Nothing will change me

Aye Jim
That's all very well
Sandra. 62. Never married.
But you can't expect someone not to change
Do you just want everyone to stay the same?
Is that what you're saying?
How can that concept even remotely be entertained
She had to change
She had to become who she needed to be
She needed to be free
You see
Nothing could stop her being free

It's a mystery of the universe
How some can wind in time
Our cells replenished every seven turns around
  the sun
Our minds embellished with every interaction
Woven factions of crystal-like distraction
Many faces
Many facets
glowing tragic pedantic tangents
Moonlit walks
As these lovers flirt

And those lovers flit
Are the ones who make it through forever unhappy?
Dreaming of something new?
Crying into their pillows at night they recite a memory
    of a brighter time
A time when he pretended to be a better man
A time when she heard his fears and took his hand
A time when he was what she wanted and her him

Or have they learned to ebb and flow
As that moon led path shows where they can go
In tandem tumbling to and fro
The odds are low
But we hope
We try
We aim for that moon drenched walk that takes us on winding routes in our forever lover's arms

---

Jo D'arc is a popular writer, musician, producer/DJ and artist currently based in Glasgow. Jo sings and plays bass guitar in The Twistettes and Girobabies and DJs as Jo Jive and the B-Hive 5. In 2021 Jo created a multi-artform project, *Minerva Wakes* which includes an album of music, visual art and a book, *Minerva and The Whir* (published by Wordville).

FRANK RAFFERTY

MY GRANNY MADE ME AN ANARCHIST

for Stuart Christie

My Granny made me an anarchist
That night when she came up with my bail.
She said: "Frankie, son, always box clever
Never let them put you into a jail."

Never let them know what you're thinking,
Or that you intend their demise,
If they stop you in the street, just keep smiling.
And remember
A smile always starts in your eyes

Read a lot, have many friends, enjoy talking,
Have a beer... or three... but never to excess
Experiment with whatever you want to
Keep in mind,
More is rarely better than less

Have sex with whoever you want to,
Who takes your fancy or you to their bed?
But try never to break any promises you've made
And keep religion well away from your head

She was just a wee wumman fae Springburn
Who claimed that she didnae know very much
But when she went into the intricacies
    of anarcho-syndicalist thought
At first I thought she was speaking in Dutch

She said there is a coming insurrection
You may not know when or where but the why
This is all that we can ever be sure of
That and the fact we all die

There's this world, there won't be another
We'll no be building new homes in the stars
Science Fiction? Keep the emphasis on fiction!
Politicians will leave you nothing but scars

They'll try to dupe you, lie to you
Don't believe them
Or their facts of the matter. It's all lies.
No matter which party they claim to stand for
They're all the same wan, with some in disguise

Now Granny never danced with Emma Goldman
Didny drink with Bakunin, Rudi Rocker or Lucy Parsons
She taught me that revolt is a natural tendency of life
And that a case may be well made for arson

Direct action said my Granny is necessity
The world can be whatever all of us create
Beyond decrees and control of parties and leaders
And there can be no redress from the state

Government isn't there for the governed
It serves the interests of the rulers and the rich
The rest of us are merely a game to be played
By those who'll never die in any ditch.

Aye, my Granny made me an anarchist
That night when she came up with my bail
She said: "Frankie, son, always box clever
Never let them put you into a jail."

———◆◆◆———

Frank Rafferty is Glaswegian, that's important. He currently lives in Derry, NI, and performs poetry and other material at various spoken word events, festivals and clubs in Ireland and the UK and is an occasional broadcaster. Frank used to be a bus conductor and he knows where you live.

THOMAS MCCOLL

50p

I was once so drunk
that, when I got home,
I fumbled round in my pocket for my key
and taking out instead a 50p
attempted to open the door with it.

You eventually came down,
thinking someone was trying to break in,
but when you realised who it was,
you let me in,
and I was so grateful,
I tried to pay you with the 50p
as if you were just some hotel maid or porter
looking for a tip.

And there you were, thinking (charitably)
it was just some kind of blip,
but recently I was once again so drunk
that when I got home
I fumbled round in my pocket for my key,
and as there just so happened to be
(on this occasion at least)
no change in my pocket to confuse me,
I found my key
but found it no longer worked.

In shock, I kept on trying the lock.
You eventually came down,
thinking someone was trying to break in,
but when you realised who it was,
you simply opened up the letterbox,
and I was so grateful,

I said: 'It's me. Could you let me in?'
But instead of letting me in,
you simply told me to 'fuck off',
and when I said, 'I live here',
you said, 'You haven't lived here for months',
and then, when I said I had no change on me
and asked if you had some to give me for the bus,
you told me again to 'fuck off',
and that, if I didn't, you'd call the police.
And with that I left
without having even been offered 50p.

And sometimes,
when I think about that,
I feel hard done by.

DEAD POP STAR

I'm 16, and my head is filled
with dreams of being a pop star—
albeit a dead one.

In fact, it's fast become
an all-consuming morbid obsession,
but with nothing for me in the 21st Century,
and being 40 years too late for new romantic,
I'm stuck with being just necromantic,
as I summon, each night, from 1981,
the most beautiful voice there was from that time—
or any time—
ideally via a (black) magic circle of vinyl
or, failing that, the demon that is digital—
and then, in my mind,
replace the pop star's name with mine,

and possess their voice, their body, their persona...
...except, of course, I don't.
All I've managed to achieve—
with this constant desire
to stay indoors and feed
on the unsettled blood that somehow flows still
through my fav dead singer's vocal cords—
is turn myself into a gaunt
and grey-faced teenage vampire...

...and, knowing I'd die in the sunlight of shame
if anyone was to ever discover the truth,
I'm forced, throughout the day,
to rein my imagination in,
wearing it like a cape of invisibility,
and it's only at night, alone in my room—
and from deep within my cranium castle—
that my imagination finally gets to fly,
swirling like a bat
with its blindsight switched on
(so that when I close my eyes I truly see).

Each night, that's what I do—
and all I ever do—
dream of being my fav dead pop star.
All the best ones are. Dead.
Why is it that everyone good is dead?
And why is it too
that some people possess amazing talent,
while some people—like me, for instance—don't?

I've all the charisma of a corpse,
whereas the corpse that is the dead pop star
somehow still has all the charisma.

At any rate, each night, while doing,
as ever, a strange, out-of-rhythm,
jerky and unfathomable dance
around my room—in a deep trance
from listening to this captured voice
on d(i)e-tunes—
I remain aware this really isn't a way to live—
living my life through someone who's dead—
but what can I do?

Whenever my favourite artist plays
(and especially when
my all-time favourite track comes on),
I live not for the present life
but for a preserved life
and, during the brief but brilliant
brass-heavy middle-eight interlude—
of an otherwise synthesized
but sensitive song—I chant:

> *I live on the blood of another—*
> *this pop star who will sing undead forever.*
> *I cannot see my face when I peer into the mirror*
> *(I'll see nothing till my dream comes true).*

Thomas McColl lives in London, and his latest collection of poetry is *Grenade Genie*, published by Fly on the Wall Press. He's performed his poetry at many events in London and beyond, including many times at Celine's Salon Soho (since his first time there in 2016), and at Celine's Salon Glasgow in April 2022.

ASHLEY CHAPMAN

FAKE, FAKIR, FLAKE

Feel empty in your post-Apocalyptic City of Angels?
Where not even your pets are real,
An android, a sheep or a frog,
The micro-electrical whir of a butterfly.

Good, and so you ought.

Now take the handles of your empathy box,
And in a shared virtual hallucination
Feel: pain, illusion, depression and despair,
The myriad outré gifts of consciousness.

Millions of discombobulated and disconnected souls,
Adam's sons; Eve's daughters
And among them simulations, too
Fakes, androids!
A phoney circuit of semi-conscious memories,
A hive of neural malaise.
Welcome to our world,
And know how dead inside I feel.

You, yes, you:

Need a pet to make you more complete?
Maybe you can afford a fake fakir flake like me who looks like Jude Law,
Sounds like Richard Burton,
And silently romances you like Rudolph Valentino.
Come and stick what's left of your mind in here.
In hair, hear her: har, har, har...

A box of lies...

A voice, Mercer's,
With texture from an age, you neither lived in nor dared in:
Al Jerry's, a TV actor,
Droning on in pre-selected tones.

The real thing, the men, the women, their animals,
Made in the wild, wild dessert, in the green pulsing savannah,
On the open crusted seas; now too, washed, choked and drained.
Too many spliced and diced mutations,
Iterating your image:
The thing that was my heart,
My child, now its imitation.

Ashley is an English ESOL teacher at Southwark College in London. He has been writing poetry and character sketches for several years with Celine's Salon in Soho and now Glasgow. *Helios Review* showcases his poetry, biography and book reviews.

KATHARINE MACFARLANE

SATURDAY NIGHT

Gonna be the best night of your life
Or at least this week's highlight
Starts like every other Saturday night before
Clothes scattered across the floor
Nothing quite right for the Best Night of Your Life
Stripped bare you don't care
Cos you're contoured to the max
Lipstick from an ad
That promised the right shade of red can turn
    dull & boring into something bold eye-catching
And tonight, this time, this is exactly
    the right shade of red
And just to be sure
You've downed a whole bottle of it
So you slide on something short & tight
It is Saturday night after all
And siren-like in the
Highest of high heels
You start the night ten feet tall
(Feet hurting like hell)
Head to the bar
Fill that half-empty glass
Bacardi Breezer or something even sweeter
    to swill out the
Strange taste of displacement
And yet it lingers
So the drinks get smaller
Shot after shot
You've still not quite got it
That easy, breezy, beautiful

Still scared, shy and somehow resentful
Of those Saturday night good timers
That seem to find it all just so easy
Another drink should ease you into it
But small talk makes you smaller
Until exhausted
Wishing the night was over
You shrink in
Drinking absinthe by yourself
Absence yourself
Like a post-Brexit Britain
Casting around desperately for a last-minute
 trade deal you settle
For something more than a little disappointing
You'd forgotten that Saturday night
Never lives up to its promises
You'd forgotten that promises never keep
You keep forgetting his name
And a tidal wave of nausea
Drowns the surging swell of shame
He's suggesting your place
Keeps breathing beer in your face
And the lines on his shirt are moving
So is his mouth but you can't hear what he's saying
Slow motion from above you watch yourself vomiting
On his really, really shiny shoes
No one moves
Then he's calling you a cow
So's that blonde girl now I think
Apparently someone spilt her drink?
I don't see how that's my problem
Stagger heavy-breathing to the bathroom
Forehead cool on the mirror
Redo eyeliner
Contouring looks shite in here
Must be the light in here

Lipstick-scrawl a question mark
On the mirror in the exact right shade of red
Half wish I was dead
Other girls worrying
Giggling
Big man saying I'm leaving
Cold
On the street
On my knees
Bacardi in reverse
I've forgotten the rest

Wake up late morning
Eyes leaking
Stomach heaves
As tongue cleaves to the roof of Sunday
Deep rapid breathing
To hold the vomit in
Breathe in
Don't dare look at my phone
No idea how I got home
Breathe in
Breathe in
I want to ink respect into my skin see it slowly sink in
But I've heard that respect only comes from within
Breathe in
Why do I need to break just to fit in?
Breathe in
Breathe in
Go back to the beginning
Breathe in
And ink love into your skin
See it slowly sink in that you've been loved from the
    very beginning

Loved even like this
Loved even this mess
Breathe in
Breathe out
Keep breathing.

ARE YOU SCARED OF DYING?

I'm sorry
Look I know it's Saturday night
We should be keeping this light and
That's not the sort of question you slide down the bar
    between pints
It's just that lately all the talk's been so small
Or crammed with chemical compounds or medical
    detail and I'm not sure I understand it all
And there are so many questions
But they all are just different shades of scared
And I probably should be more prepared.
I know this is the talk we haven't dared have yet
We're not just musing hypothetically on life's fragility
    or our own mortality
This time it's real
And I really don't know how you feel...
I mean when you close your eyes and think about
    death is it a big guy, dressed in black, maybe on horseback
    carrying a scythe?
Is death already part of your life?
Do you know it as a blessed relief like a warm breeze
    on a beach or a friend walking beside you but
    just out of reach
Oh god I sound like a hallmark card
I knew this was going to be hard
I've watched you fighting it
Calm as the needles sink in

Breathing through radiation
Joking that you always knew you needed therapy
Just hadn't imagined it'd be the chemo variety
Are you afraid of dying or are you ready for death?
For weeks
This question has stung stuck on my lips
conversation choked past it
every word framed around it as it hangs between us
This question asked easily so many times before
Are you scared?
Exam scared, first date scared, end of the aisle scared,
    labour ward scared
Are you scared?
We have shared everything.
And you were always prepared
always had the answers or a book for it;
The wedding planner, Gina Ford,
But what book do I get you now?
The art of dying
The last words
Or simply one on how not to cry
Cos we've come too far now together to cry uncle
Too far to cry at all
We both learned when we were small that crying
    doesn't fix anything at all
And I don't need to see tears to know where it hurts
Your scars say it all
Scarred but you never seem scared.
We have all seen your strength
Seen your dignity
Unafraid of your own fragility
You have been all I know I could never be
So tell me, are you scared?
Because I am terrified
Terrified that we might be out together tonight
    for the last time

Terrified each time that this time might be
    the last time
Too scared to eat
Too scared to sleep
Too scared to leave your side
I am terrified
Knowing death will come calling
And you'll ask me to keep breathing.

Katharine Macfarlane is an award-winning Skye-based poet, writer, workshop facilitator and ex-Children and Young People's Librarian. She is the 2020 Scottish Slam Champion.

PINKY

DUAL PARTS

We stayed late tonight,
I never tire of your voice.
As the mirror ball crowned parts of your sound;
Grazing sparkles that hit
the lipstick stains on my wine glass.
Homeward bound in your presence.
Reeling at the notion
Of how one man envelops
Future, past and present.
Mapping me in a crest of waves and four walls
At the same time.
I'm half the woman I used to be,
Till betrothed to you.
Not for rhyme nor reason
Will another hang my moon
For you've pinned stars in forgotten places
Scattered at Creation;
No myth, religion, God or darkness can consume.
Not dawn nor day
Remember us the way we do.
Our never-ending story,
Our endless embrace,
The deathless vow.
For the way I loved you then,
I love you now.

Hannah (AKA Pinky) came from Brighton to Soho. A hairstylist and rapscallion, she has been writing creatively and cathartically since six. She says she's humbled to have support of Celine's Salon and close friends, and to contribute her poetry to this volume.

MARIA BEADELL

THE BALLAD OF THE HIGH PRIESTESS

Buds in bloom, full of promise
The cold is gone and here comes the spring.

Dawning sun heralds the future.
I am your Queen, and you are my King.

But ripped away, torn away
Blown to pieces and left to decay.

I am cruelly cast aside
And this is how it turns, the tide

My hopes and dreams cruelly dashed
You pierced my heart and my crown, you smashed.

But rise again I will and find my way
The sun will not set on *me* this day.

And there I was, breathing, thriving, feeling
Punished I will be, for my own ancestral healing.

They resent me for my knowing, my faith, my blood
So they kick me down and drag me through the mud

Defile my body, then burn it in flame
'Til no one shall even remember my name.

Kill me then, kill me you must!
Shatter my bones into the dust.

And for what? The bitterness, the envy, the rage
A war against women you will wage

Revenge against mothers who weren't there?
The burden that all women must now bear

Victims of man's resentment and fear
Well, our destruction will cost you dear.

I am the High Priestess, all that's wise and true
Comes from me, but is also, in *you*.

I stand here defiant; my body is mine.
I will not apologise, for I have committed no crime.

I will not hide the pain or the grief;
The faith, the love, the unwavering belief.

I will not mask the messy part,
My tears, my blood, my wounded heart.

I am not ashamed of my softness, nor my steel.
My capacity for love, or my ability to heal.

I celebrate my body, I celebrate my soul
I am one, and I am whole.

I deserve to be heard; I deserve to be seen
For all that I am and for all that I've been.

Like a phoenix, emerging from the flame,
I am the High Priestess, and **I rise again**.

Maria is a writer, painter and performer. She runs her own theatrical walking tour company dedicated to telling women's stories called Herstorical Tours.

MARK MCGHEE

LAST MAN STANDING ON THE EDGE OF THE WORLD
lyrics

I'm sorry but I got it, they got me, am going
On a faraway holiday no plan on returning.
Would you miss me? Lately, I ain't so sure
From soothsayer to noo dour I no longer feel truer
And you are levitating over me and pure
Am a footnote of an anecdote but the future needs you
I've become a worser version of my former person
Denial gives permission to pick up this weapon
Reality cheats me and leads to aggression
Want to break out this box that am stuffed down
    and kept in
I reckon the dirt road just got too damn windy
The twists were confusing the lights how they blind me
Satnavs to enemies mapped out how they find me
In unlikely hidey holes, me? Me! me no likey.
I am leaving a trail I'm too tired to fight it
Stole petrol from Peter told Paul to ignite it.

    Last Man standing on the edge of the world
    Rolling solo with a flag unfurled.

This is a man who runs from discussion
Comes from the tunnel of fuzz and expulsion
Turns into devil on worst of consumption
Struggles to function and fucking disgusting
Understands why you can't but just wants you to love him
Outcast from all funding relies on his cunning
I speak in the third I see some of you wondering
Looking for the forks in the tongue in abundance

It sickens to witness the pits of corruption
The worst bits conforming in order to summon
Up a little something I'm burnt out but gunning
For those who forbid me, forgive me, am coming
But you can't stun me with a lump sum
Am troublesome and running
Onto oncoming traffic with a mask made for surgeon
The muzzle hides a piece of the puzzle called consumption
Translating isolation but transmitting from nothing.

> Last Man standing on the edge of the world
> Rolling solo with a flag unfurled.

Mark McGhee is a Glaswegian writer, musician and broadcaster. He is the lead singer of two popular bands: Jackal Trades and Girobabies and runs an irreverent online show about culture called You Call That Radio. *Last Man Standing on the Edge of the World* is from Jackal Trades' latest album, *At This Point*.

PART TWO

Céline's Derry Salon

Frank Rafferty
Michael Groce
Mel Bradley
Valerie Bryce
Keiran Goddard
Ronan Carr
PBJ
Niall O'Mianain
Juanita Rea
George Houston
James King And Ann McKay

FRANK RAFFERTY

YOUR HEALTH

for our NHS

My grandparents could barely breathe from
 tightening their belts,
It's hard now to imagine all the terror which they felt
Each time when they or one of theirs was sick
 or taken ill,
Could they afford the medicine? The £2 doctor's bill?

YET each and every time today, when families
 are unwell.
Health care is free, for her, for me. Now there's a
 tale to tell!
You grant me that serenity which they had
 never known,
From their collective will you sprang,
 completely ours, home grown.

My Dad's sister Patricia, she was the aunt we'd
 never meet,
Back then pneumonia often brought a funeral
 to the street.
But no magic spell did summon you,
 you are our own creation.
You were demanded ... and out you came ... from
 post war devastation.

You embody love for everyone... and still
 we understate
Your true value and your worth to us, since 1948.
You grant me the serenity that those before me
 had not known.
From their collective will you sprang,
 completely ours, home grown.

If and when we can we pay so that if and when
    there's need;
By her, by me, by neighbours, strangers, friends
    ... you'll intercede,
With doctors, nurses, hospitals, new treatments
    for our pain.
You act as salve and balm when we are wounded or insane.

We'll never know, because of you, the fear people once felt.
Poor people who could barely breathe from
    tightening their belts.
You grant me the serenity which they had never known
From their collective will you sprang,
    completely ours, home grown.

TEMPLEMORE

for the peace, written on the morning of day 666 of no NI Assembly—the last time

Not pretending to understand.
I've no idea at all.
Some years ago, on an election night.
They came in and they cleared out the hall.

Outside folk stood, chatting and smoking
I thought you were taking the hand.
You said there might be a bomb in the car park...
I said: "What The Fuck..?"
Then I ran
.... when I realised that you weren't joking
I jogged on, off over that field.
The rest of you stood there, laughing and smoking.
I couldn't believe this was real.
How could that ever seem normal?
I ran. Yes, I did. And so what?
My heart was just battering my chest out
My stomach was an aching, tight knot.

Back home, I went into his bedroom
I sat there, just breathing my fear.
His head fast asleep, on the pillow.
Why has this all happened here?

And as I sat, so quiet in that darkness,
A gulp down deep into my throat.
I thought of that story you told me
Of the wee boy who died, on that boat.

A boy just enjoying the summer.
At work, never thinking he'd die
And the two of you, waving down from the headland,
Under a blazing blue sky.
All that wreckage, all those hearts torn asunder.
All those people, all those lives, your poor friend.
All that madness, all that utter destruction.
Yet somehow, you've made it all, nearly end.

Later, I'm still sat there. Not sleeping.
Then a sound, from the distance, from the dark
Kind of a... WHUUUMPF!   An explosion?
You only wake up when the dogs start to bark.

MICHAEL GROCE

LET THE GUINNESS FLOW

Let the Guinness flow my friend
The black and white together
For the history of our paths
Will be entwined forever

From the Irish seas
To the Celtic shores
Distant roots of Mother Africa
Is the inspiration for our source

For we tell the same story
Same story we tell daughters and sons
As we recollected and ponder
About the negative things that have been done

For we hear the painful cries of slavery
Smell the death of freedom wars
As so many of our people
Bravely died for the cause

As they crossed the Atlantic
Many became victims of the sea
They would gaze towards the motherlands
As returning home becomes the dream

The Irish voices kept on singing
The Irish music kept on playing
The Irish feet kept on dancing
Let the Guinness flow

Afro drums kept on drumming
Afro hearts kept on pumping
The Afro feet kept on dancing
Let the Guinness flow

Let the Guinness flow my friend
The black and white together
For the history of our paths
Will be entwined forever

Michael Groce is a multi-award winning and BBC Windrush Poet.

MEL BRADLEY

FEARLESSNESS

To me, you are the feeling of five.

That magical invincibility of
rushing downhill no brakes.
Mouth open. Sounds thumping
up from my chest, punctuated
by the blunt slap, slap, slap of
foot to path. Momentum harnessed.
Arms thrown wide to the world. Chest free.
Embracing the air like it was a friend
not seen in forever. Without thought
or care of feet losing their ability to
sequence and tumbling. Thudding
back to earth, teeth-marked sore tongue
and bloodied nose.

Best-friends taking turns at 'protector-ing'
in the dark of night-time sleeps.
Safely tucked up in each other's arms
away from the dreaded edge-of-the-bed
monster that my past adult life warns,
all waggy-finger and scorn-face to be
careful of. Elbow to fingertips
distance is safe. But you,
you taunt the edge.

Because you are untouchable!
And I love being securely curled up
against your spine, holding tight
until it's safe enough to let go.

You are my five.

Mel Bradley is a spoken word artist, writer, burlesque and drag performer, theatre-maker, actor, multimedia artist, designer, general show-off/know-it-all creative genius with the attention span of a gnat with over 10 years of writing for performance experience. She is an unapologetically outspoken queer feminist performer with a candid voice and an unhealthy obsession with the Virgin Mary.

VALERIE BRYCE

SWAN LAKE

Thomas Friel, locally known as 'Panache'
Was said to be heavy footed
By virtue of the fact that all his thinking
Had fallen south of his head.
Thomas had been a source of amusement
Since his First Holy Communion
When his slow shuffle to the altar
Was accompanied by a sound not unlike a walrus
Or a seal…a prank by an older boy
Thoroughly enjoyed by a sniggering congregation.
His life henceforth became a series
Of mishaps and non-events
Retold again and again
As though to rubber stamp the town's knowledge
That he was an idiot.
His face and hair and clothes responded in kind
As earthly things do
Hanging lower with each passing year.
A longing for freedom, elegance, companionship
Drove him to feed a kitchen stool
Through the pantry window
And gallop down the bray
Towards the lake
To meet the swans half way
In flight.
A stillness fell upon his poet's soul
As he breathed in their magnificence
Sheer delight that they'd respond in kind
As spirit things do
To one who would balance
Two feet off the ground
To join them.

He surrendered to the swirling flurry
Felt his heartbeat in rhythm
With their white feathered wings
Welcomed their acceptance of him
Full sure they were his kin.
'I'll come back as one of ye' he said.
And there was more lightness
In that moment at the lakeside
Than the townspeople could ever comprehend.

THE THREADS OUR HEARTS WEAVE

Invisible to the human eye
Silk threads weave round and about
Our giving and receiving.
Pool in moments we may not notice
A smile, patience, compassion
All imprinting felt colours.
The orange of a warm belly
Filled with gratitude and a cooked meal.
The deepest blue of safety
Child's buggy lifted from the train.
A blood red of presence, a squeezed hand
During times of indescribable pain.
These threads weave again and again
Until all the world is covered
In a fragile mesh.
The silver of young children and dogs
Almost visible in their skin or fur
Indisputable, unconditional wonder
Glinting because you are their sun
And you smile back a whole sea of yellow threads.
Summer field green dotted with wildflowers
In the stillness of a silent moment between friends

An expression of intuition and wisdom and love
Where words would have failed.
'Look for the helpers' we tell our young
When they grow to walk the places
Where kindness looks far from reach.
For they must first bear witness
White synapses firing
And heart pulsating
Responding to the truth that everywhere
Everywhere
There is kindness to be found
And felt.
And it is ok to fill yourself up with it!
To accept the kaleidoscope of colours
Swirling through your cells
To let them sit a while
Weaving their tapestry of your own personal
    expression.
Until out through your mouth, your eyes
Your hands, your whole being
Burst the threads of gold
Healing manuka honey
For the soul
The thread that connects us to each other
And to our own divinity.

Valerie Bryce is a poet, activist and cultural events organiser living in Letterkenny in the beautiful county of Donegal, Ireland. Valerie's work is concerned with exploring the link between the human body, nature and spirituality and reclaiming ourselves from the binds imposed by unjust societal norms and practices.

KEIRAN GODDARD

FOR RICHER, FOR POORER

I solemnly swear;
I will peel back the bandage
and let all of your pollen lift.

With clean hands I will work
the blue-gold pelt of you
until it is just soft enough to split.

I will reach in and search
for the simple dead things
old muscle and tissue and bone.

I'll drink all my fil,
I'll sew and then bathe you
and tie up the thread at the end of the wound.

And I'll count down from twenty
and untangle the knot
and tear you again where the grace of things bloomed.

Keiran Goddard is from Shard End, Birmingham and was educated at the University of Oxford. The author of one poetry pamphlet *Strings* and two full-length poetry collections *For The Chorus* and *Votive*, his debut collection was shortlisted for the Melita Hulme Prize and he was the runner up in the William Blake Prize. He speaks internationally on issues related to social change and currently develops research on workers' rights, automation and trade unionism. His debut novel, *Hourglass*, published by Little Brown, has been longlisted for the Desmond Elliott Prize.

RONAN CARR

PAUL MULDOON
lyrics

First among greats was W B Yeats
Spinnin' linguistic plates
For his Celtic Twilight Mates
(He's a poet and he knows it
He's no baboon)

Seamus Heaney raised a glass to the Queenie
With words he was no Meany
So he made a-lots-a greeny
(He's a poet and he knows it
He's no buffoon.)

> *Chorus*
> He's a poet and he knows it
> Just like Paul Muldooooon
> Reaching for his plume
> In the month of June
> As he considers the moon
> Cause that's what poets do

You know who's extremely nice
It's that Colette Bryce
She'll stay up all night
Making the line good and tight.
(She's a poet and she knows it
Just like that Green Fool.)

But guess who said 'feck it'
It was Samuel Beckett
A rhyme he tried to perfect it
But his head he just-a-wrecked it
(He's no poet and he knows it
He's no Muldoon)

> *Chorus*
> He's a poet and he knows it
> Just like Paul Muldooooon
> So languid and measured
> He'll rhyme for your pleasure
> In his pin-striped trouser-suit
> Cause that's what poets do
>
> (*spoken*) Yeah that's what they do
> They get themselves into rhyming situations
> And they write it all down

Medbh McGuckian
Cookin chicken an' onion
In Seamus Deane's oven
At gas mark Seven

Patrick Kavanagh
Wasn't haven it
With the mot from Ranelagh
So he took to his drinks cabinet

Paul Meehan
Had a crazy old dream
About Speranza and Behan
On a drinking spree
(All Poets and they know it
All Beautiful)

All Poets and they know it
Just like Paul Muldooon
Reaching for his plume
In the month of June
As he considers the moon
Cause that's what the poets doo hoo hoo hoo....

Ronan Carr is an award-winning actor/writer from Dublin whose plays have been seen in Dublin, London, New York and Derry. He has written screenplays for shorts, *Coolockland*, and features, *Rewind*. Ronan has had great success as a radio dramatist for the Irish national broadcaster RTÉ with dramas such as *To Sean with Love*. He co-founded his own company Mockingbird Theatre and is currently in rehearsal with his new play *Down by The River Sáile*; which is about Hollywood icon Jane Russell and the Irish mother whose baby she adopted.

PBJ

MY LAST WILL AND TESTAMENT

When I go
It is optional
If you wanna
See me one
Last time

Just let
Them
Burn me

When I go
I do not
Want a wake
Or even a
Funeral

I am pretty
Sure you can
Find something
Better to do
For three days

Just remember me
For the rest
Of your lifetime
The way you
Wanna remember me

As I pull
Out a bus
Ticket
In a busy
City

Realising
The power of
A piece of
Paper

Like
A young man
Surviving a car
Crash
Behind Us

WRITING IS DANGEROUS

Writing is a dangerous act

I open a box of paperclips
I don't notice I've cut myself

I see the blood smudged
On the page a minute later

I take a minute to think

It is as dangerous as
The first time you say *I love you*

ANONYMOUS

It's a shame
I haven't felt close
To someone in years

Maybe there is
An angel up there
Somewhere

Singing a song of love
That will last me
Forever

PBJ is a published poet and a columnist for the International Times. The BBC published his first story and The Playhouse in Derry screened his first film.

NIALL O'MIANAIN

CRAIC ADDICT

I'm a craic addict,
flat at it,
not admit it, stuck in it, live it and repeat it

Repeat it and live, voices scream: give into
submission, summon craic to attention, forget
where you've come from,
the sesh is your new home.
I'd better call for forgiveness or I'm going to regret
this
but sure
fuck it I'm in it,
Spin ethereal bliss, blast beautiful mist, ignore my
daily abyss; and its delicate twist...

That this is a tale of admission,
come listen and learn some
on my habitual condition—it's clear that I'm itching
this addiction of craic
Yet I fear I am missing my last year with my dad—
he's been diagnosed with cancer
I've been turning my back, summoning craic, afraid
of the fact
that I'll fracture and crack
if I speak with my da
about his final hurrah; real shit.

Open my eyes and believe it,
love him before he leaves it.
Praise God while he needs it,
Da, I love you I mean it.
Believe in myself and become it.

This is love and I miss it,
You're at home and I'm missing,
Gone ten days a week, not messing.
Partying flat the tin,
it's a sin,
you're at home all alone while I'm out acting
the partying drone, thinking I own the throne,
when I'm nobody's wandering gnome,
slowly going insane,
repeating the same mistakes again,
same shit different pen.

Can't pretend to care when things are so fucked up at
home and I'm not even there,
and I swear I'll change, and I know I won't,
and this isn't a game and I'm losing hope...

I'm smoking dope and swinging boats,
The craic's afloat and I'm trapped on board
And I can't escape, it's a great mistake.
It's a hell-bound place and we ain't slowing pace
And my life is bait on a string called fate
and these waves ain't great,

Got me breaking my faith,
now these demons await,
they're gonna take me away,
please pray, pray, pray for me,
help me to see a way of breaking free from smoking
weed has broken me,
minds in need of sobriety,
the irony is, Da,
you're the key to open up my flood gates, generate this love sate,
I seriously need to meditate and question why I think it's great
to wake and bake
and waste my day,
the craic is great
but man
it takes its toll.

Niall O'Mianain is a rhyme enthusiast with devilish flow, focusing on storytelling's communal soul. A Derry-based performer boasting accents all over and nowhere will save your applauding surrender.

JUANITA REA

FEARLESS

She can dive into dark oceans
and fall weightless through the sky,
she's been tossed in raging rivers
cos she wants to be fearless, fearless.

Yet it's been hard for her to go back
and face shadows from her past
and they're cast into her arms and legs
still she wants to be fearless, fearless.

I've seen her run, I've seen her falter
I've seen her float into the mist
she stands here now bleeding and broken
just aching to be kissed.
She is ripped up and she is open.
She cannot run, she cannot hide.
Standing, falling, bleeding, breaking,
just aching to be kissed.

These are my arms, my legs, my body
I will not run, I will not hide.
I bleed, I break my softness heals me.
I know I'm not fearless, fearless.

This is my ache, this is my longing
to touch, to hold, to kiss, to dance.
Feeling, falling, tingling, trembling
terrified and fearless, fearless.

I will not run, though I will falter.
At times I float into the mist.
I stand here now bleeding and broken
just aching to be kissed.
I am ripped up and I am open
I cannot run, I cannot hide.
Standing, falling, bleeding, breaking,
just aching to be kissed.

Standing, falling, bleeding, breaking,
just aching to be kissed.

Juanita Rea is a South African Indian interdisciplinary artivist, de-stigmatising childhood sexual abuse and mental disorders through the combined arts while facilitating community arts and wellbeing programmes, particularly for the underserved. She is a Visiting Scholar at Queen's University Belfast.

GEORGE HOUSTON

HONEYSUCKLE

lyrics

Honeysuckle, Honeysuckle
Where is my bed?
I'll pay you half a ha'penny
To soothe my weary head

Honeysuckle, Honeysuckle
Sing me off to sleep
I'll pay you many cherries and
The red ones don't come cheap

Honeysuckle, Honeysuckle
Sticking to my lip
I'll steal but one more kiss from you
For one more syrup sip

Honeysuckle, Honeysuckle
Laying on the bed
Of grass so green and pearly
My Darling, dearest, dead

MISTY EYES

Those portal windows to the soul
Whose mist and fog push up the pain
In secret hides the truths you hold
Through one-way glass she reaches out
To pull you in. Drenched by cloud
The air is matt and ice as thin
As spindles I'm suspended by
I'm on the outside looking in
The cold soul's window
Misty eyes

ROSES

lyrics

I get it
I would fuck him too
He's gorgeous
More just like those princes
That they write about in stories

He smiles with cheek
His eyes are green
They've seen more of you
Than I've ever seen
And I bet you beg them more please

I could never blame you for having eyes
He turned my head when I first saw him
By the sidewalk in my mind
I thought another teenage heartthrob
I could never blame you for living life
I always pictured you so happy
In the corner of my mind's eye
I seen so

I always pictured you with me though

You get the husband
He gets the job
Works nine to five n' comes home a slob
Feed the children and the dog

Each Valentine's a new bouquet of roses
Withered and decayed
Hit the sack 'cause he's okay
Another year done trying

I always seen you with that smile
In stupid visions of the future
I thought that once you could be mine
But never knew just how to treat you

So, I see you with your grin
We're in the future now you're golden
'Cause you're with him and I'm the old one
That was the smile that I'd hold on to
In the corner of my mind's eye
I seen so

I always pictured you with me though

I get it
I would love him too
He's gorgeous
More just like those princes
That they write about in stories

George Houston is a singer songwriter from Inishowen, Donegal. Always trying to prioritise the narrative of each song, he allows a wide range of genres and styles to embody the stories he sings about.

JAMES KING AND ANN MCKAY

HIGHS AND SIGHS AND ICE SAD EYES

"In the same way as the mind wanders hither and
thither the back seizes up and immobilises."

        hint this aim whey has demand want hers hit her
          hand the there dip hag sees his hub hand
              hymn owe bill eyes his

hand her his eyes
I sander sighs
ice and her sand high high
high handed sighs eye her sand
high handed eyes sighed hi
highs and sighs hi highs and sighs
highs and sighs and ice sad eyes

      Highs and sighs and ice sad eyes ...
      No getting away from the ice,   ,
      no matter how the fools carry on,
      fooling only themselves that life's a laugh,
      a tall story accessed by beanstalk,
      denouement loaded with bagged gold, exoneration,
      all kinds of love.
      You know this story.
      You were that fool.
      Now you've wound your neck in.
      In your constricted throat dry beans
      fail to germinate, disintegrate.
      You swallow dust, you sigh.

The golden land has dulled and paled—
before your eyes, it silvers, ices over.
You view the fools through frosted lenses.
They eye the sky—and jump.

James King has performed here and there for about fifty years.
Ann McKay is happy to be a pensioner, alive and creating.

PART THREE

Ros Moore
Celine Hispiche
Susie Wild
Heather Moulson
Kevin O'Dowd
Billy Parker
Anonymous
Siobhan Lancaster
Nerys Beattie
Bob Reeves

ROS MOORE

DINBYCH Y PYSGOD...

Dinbych y Pysgod ond wyt ti mor hardd
Yn estyn a disgyn fel geiriau y bardd

Dros cregyn a cherrig yn codi mae'r môr
Y llanw o'n amgylch yn canu fel côr.

Wrth ymadael siop Greggs gyda pasti 'n fy llaw
Dw i'n gwybod bod gwylan yn sbïo pen draw.

Mor sydyn mae'n disgyn o'r cwmwl uwchben
Yn dwgid y pasti gan hedfan i'r nen.

Cer o ma'r hen lleidr, Dim ffrind da ti nawr
Yn dychryn fy nerfau a'th d'adain mor fawr

Dros cregyn a cherrig yn codi mae'r môr
Gwylanod yn sgrechian ymatab i'r côr.

O Dinbych y pysgod ond wyt ti mor hardd
Yn disgyn ac estyn fel geiriau y bardd.

...TENBY

O Tenby. But you are so beautiful
Rising and falling like the words of a poet.
Over shells and stones the seas rise
The tide around us sings like a choir.

On leaving Greggs
With a PASTIE in hand
I am aware that a seagull
is spying on me.

Suddenly he descends
From the cloud above
Stealing the pastie
And flying off to heaven.

Clear off you old thief
I am no friend of yours
Playing on my nerves
With your gigantic wings

Over shells and stones
The sea passes
Seagulls scream
In response to the choir

O Tenby
But you are so beautiful
Rising and falling
As do the words of a poet.

TENBY TUESDAY—BEFORE DAWN

I was driven to follow my intuition
Walking the distance between
Waiting for the night sky to wake
The new day
Willing the box to open
Without success
Turning from my entrance door
Some forty feet above the beach
Weaving my way
Behind the building
I descend the steps with trepidation.
I step onto dimly lit sand
Sharing speckled grains of moonlight with dawn's incoming might
Still shadowed by the night.
Then it happens.
I STAND IN AWE.

This raspberry smoothie of a sea
This bath of blood
INVADES MY BEING
IT MAKES ME WHOLE
I know I was led here this Tenby morn
I understand the purpose of it all.
I EXPERIENCE
CREATION
Turning towards home I ascend the twenty steps
Transcend the boarded walkway
To my dwelling
Flicking open the key box
The code clicks into action.
I retrieve the key
With ease.

"Follow your intuition"
Her words
Now echo
In my heart
"It will serve you well"

SONG OF THE TIMES

lyrics

Let us live without a newsreel
Darkening our thoughts
Men in power playing games
Until at last they're caught
Playing games and changing lanes
Are skills that we are taught.

Pan fo'r byd yn colli enaid
(When the world loses its soul / spirit)
Ride above the clouds
Cymer cam ar gyfer pawb
(Take a step on behalf of all)
Teulu'r byd, ein chwaer a brawd
(The world / family our sister and brother)
Share a hope and make a plan
Gobaith nawr sydd yn y man
(There is hope in place)

Instrumental

Chwarae gemau—plant i gyd
(Playing games—children ... all of them)
In a world with so much greed
Take a chance and sew the seed

Instrumental

Gad i bawb dod ati 'nghyd
(Let's all join together)

Born in Wales, Ros grew up in the Welsh tradition of performing in Eisteddfods where culture is expressed through music, poetry, theatre, dance and the arts. Her work is performance-based poetry, prose, song and script, often bi-lingual. A professional singer crossing the genres of music she has a passion for Latin, swing and jazz, performing these in English, Welsh, French, Spanish and Italian. Many of the jazz classics she has translated into Welsh and has performed them live on Welsh television and radio.

CELINE HISPICHE

CURIOSITIES

In memory of the lost Tenby Lifeboat Men

Let the sea pull in
Stories of the night
Let the waves unroll
Their magic to recite

Let the rocks encase
Deep secret passages
Burning gas lights
Fall on darken carriages

Let the air around
Form a wordsmith mist
Laying on your tongue
A taste you can't resist

A salty frothy richness
Flows like gushing water
A story-telling folly
Ink ground in pestle and mortar…

There's a storm a-brewing
And the boats just made it in
The pipes howl in the wind
And the nets are wearing thin

They'll end up in the sluice
Broken oars and torn rafters
And the ones that turned over?
Lay to rest for ever after

And the courage of the men
Whose jackets made of cork
Lower their lanterns
And turn to the lightning fork

And the wives they do er' cry
To the whistling of the wind
And the angels' lullaby
Sings out to their kin

For the sea has many secrets
Resting on its bed
Gone are many people
Whose sweat and courage bled

The rocks hold many scars
Hard cracking indentation
From boats that came afar
In search of a new nation

Rope knots are a-creaking
Sea slapping on their backs
For a wealth they are er' seeking
To mark their beaten tracks

And hidden on the seabed
A pot of bravery gold
And gone is their weeping
For they are fearless and bold

Like serpents they dive deep
And fill their pockets full
This is theirs to keep
Their courage conquers all

Yes, you have the courage
Oh brave men of the night

Yes, this is a salute to you
My thoughts are held so tight

Yes, I doff my cap to you
Oh heroes of the ocean

Yes, I light a candle bright
For my gratitude is spoken

SUSIE WILD

EVERYONE GOT MARRIED

He was a cupped hand
to the cigarettes she'd quit

but taken up again, only to burn
the time they spent like candles.

She cast lines and nets,
caught wishes,

the glint of beaked mackerel,
the silver lining to a flesh-pecked bone.

Beyond their boat, stars were strung
across the late sky:

bauble-eyed, they tried
to drop anchor.

CAR WHEELS ON A GRAVEL ROAD

After Lucinda Williams

We are in the car—Gibson on the backseat,
cwtched with our stage hats and dusty bags—
as we take a ride through the mizzle, along
the A470. Waterfalls and jawdrop views fly by,
familiar—still favourites, we *know* this road
and I lean back, my cowboy-boot-shod feet up
on the dashboard. The city crying dirt behind us.
Loretta's singing on the stereo. Waylon
Jennings and John Prine. We gallop
towards mountains, a first pint, the next gig.
Got folks in Llani we're gonna meet.

I LIKE YOUR FACE

he said, but please excuse mine
I have been burning the candle
at both ends, and now it is a melt
of wax, but you can place your thumb
prints here and here, claim me
as your own, if you'd like. Mostly
I'm not malleable, but fully formed,
yet there's room, at the soft edge
of things. There's room, for you.

WILD FLOWERS

Now when we come together,
we splinter bones.

Our mirrored injuries
bloom across our feet,

as we find weight too hard to bear.
Outside September rays

have willed one surviving
sunflower tall, a spike of petals unfurls.

Two magpies chatter amongst the apples
still clinging to the tree.

The lawn, I've given up on,
burgeons pink with wild

strawberries, yellow with dandelion
like ripped knickers strewn

beneath the unseasonable laundry
strung out to dry.

Inside he watches the boxing
to distract from his pain,

waiting for petals
to break through the skin.

WINDFALLS

Next door's apples now overhang
the garden fence above the sunspot
where I sit and read in the afternoon.

The boughs heavy with fruit flushed
by the heatwave, dropping like flies as I watch,
ignoring the piles of bills before me.

Though tomato plants shoot
taller and taller, blossoming
yellow, new flowers
still wilt in the corner.

I imagine sitting at the table later,
being rained on; each apple
a small bomb.

The patchy grass, the path, the veg beds
are drowning in windfalls
alive with insect feeding and decay.

Susie Wild is author of the poetry collections *Windfalls* and *Better Houses*, the short story collection *The Art of Contraception* listed for the Edge Hill Prize, and the novella *Arrivals*. Her work has recently featured in Carol Ann Duffy's pandemic project WRITE Where We Are NOW, *The Atlanta Review*, *Ink, Sweat & Tears* and *Poetry Wales*. She has placed in competitions including the Welshpool Poetry Festival Competition, the Prole Laureate Prize and the Mslexia Women's Poetry Competition and performed at festivals including The Laugharne Weekend, Green Man and Glastonbury. She lives at the bottom of a mountain in south Wales.

HEATHER MOULSON

YOURS

When you smashed the fag machine
I felt a spark between us
So, let's go back to yours!

You're not like those college boys—
Pogo sticking, purple Mohicans.
A load of posh bores!

I don't want someone like them
But you'll want someone like me
One who drops her drawers!

The Police want to talk to you
And you'll be barred—again
So, we'll do it outdoors!

I'll put on me magenta lipstick
It'll match your purple flares
And we'll do it on all fours!

JUST ANOTHER SCRUBBER

What are you doing now, you daft cow?! You never talk! Why don't you say something?! You won't get a boyfriend, you know; they'll pass you by if you're shy. They like you to talk to them, don't they?! I've not even held a boy's hand, are they bonier than a girl's? Hairier, Maureen says. And you have to kiss them if they walk you home. You snogged someone at the school disco, you know what it's like. Even though they legged it afterwards. If they put their tongue in your mouth, that means they want to Have It Away with you. And you can catch VD off a boy if he fingers you with dirty nails. Or if you sit on a public bog. So, you'd better watch it. Julie Street says it hurts the first time but she's talking out her arse! Who would do it with her?! She's disgusting. Bulging out of her school skirt, says she's up the spout! Bloody Liar! Janet Beck's got spots from Having It Away too much. Scrubber. I'd love to ask her what it's like when a boy pulls your knickers down. So bloody embarrassing, like when Mr Hodge looked at my jumper. And to think you have to talk to them too. And what if you get pregnant off them?! Would you have to marry them?! Fancy your Mum and Dad knowing you've done it with a boy. Me aunties and uncles looking at me, no wedding night nerves for her, they'd nudge each other if I turned up in white. Oh Lord, I'd be just another scrubber!

PUNK PANTOUM — 77

Why have you dyed your hair blue?!
Aren't those safety pins painful?
Stop giving Woolworths aggravation
For banning that Pistols record.

Aren't those safety pins painful?
Stop slagging off the Queen
For banning that Pistols record.
Face it, bondage just isn't you.

Stop slagging off the Queen.
Light up one of your 20 Kensitas
Face it, bondage just isn't you
We'll listen to Leo Sayer's LP.

Light up one of your 20 Kensitas
We'll toast the silver jubilee
We'll listen to Leo Sayer's LP
You really are shit at pogo sticking

We'll toast the silver jubilee
Stop giving Woolworths aggravation
You really are shit at pogo sticking
Why have you dyed your hair blue?!

Heather co-founded Poetry Performance in Teddington in 2017 and has been writing poetry ever since. She has performed extensively in London, particularly Celine's Salon and Soho Poets. Her debut pamphlet *Bunty, I Miss You* was published in 2019. Heather won the Brian Dempsey Memorial Award in 2020. Heather also writes reviews and obsessively sketches her black cat.

KEVIN O'DOWD

TALK AIN'T CHEAP

Clever words are spoken
Full of passion not of need
A love divorced of any reason
In a world that teaches greed.

Grab the flames that flicker
You could burn, you may consume
Grab the flames that flicker
They may well lead you to the truth.

But then what is the truth in this a perfect world?
A world where problems don't occur
So does that mean you won't feel no pain
And I won't feel no hurt?

And what of love? I may well ask.
Doesn't love run blind?
And we'll forgive, we won't forget
Because in the end we're all the same.
We'll say whatever seems to be
The safest bloody bet.

Kevin O'Dowd is a self-taught fashion designer who specialises in designing and hand embellishing/ embroidering stage outfits for pop stars. He is currently writing lyrics with music producer Man Parrish. He also writes and performs poetry and slam poetry.

BILLY PARKER

brain flaps
flapping
flappers flapping
flop
flip
flop
climb inside and dig
through the flaps
through the flops
to find
flipping everything

i wish i could see through the holes in the backs of your eyes which

i want to climb through
climb into
and flap around in my flip flops
as
fools flap
and
fools fall
and
i think i need a wall

you don't have walls where you need them

i've got walls in all the wrong places

and
fools
fall
but
fooling falls are fucked up for god's sake
but you are the right kind of fool
a foolish fool none the less
a fool that flip flops through the flaps
as i dig
trying to excavate everything
flapping around until i can find something
but i can find nothing
i can't find anything
and i want to trip
and
fall
down
into
a foolish fool
but none the less
fall further than any fool has fallen
before
so that i can see your atoms

your atoms
your atoms
atoms
atoms

and

rolling to the back of my brain
under the flaps
flapping flappers
flappers fucking
fucking fuckers

it's rude to swear
smoke over there
i can smoke where i want
can do whatever you want
i can't

    What are you thinking about?
An elephant grows and a whale shrinks as the air breathes and the water sinks and when and what and where become one but separate in the cloudy air of past and present and future which are all actually the same but how can they be for i know not the events of the future apart from in dreams and it is in dreams and only in dreams that the reality of nature is revealed for the subconscious is free from the suffocations of society it is society that kills people not people people are just wood and metal and trees and bones and fossils and fire and love is just particles that want to combine in an attempt to make sense of the unsensical non reality that we live in and death is just end to the despair of life end to the endless thinking about what is and what could and what should and what wants to be be and death is rebirth and rebirth is love and love is death and love is what because i don't know because love is fake or is it real or is it sex or is it kneeling before a god constructed of atoms rather than a god constructed of dreaming and god is just a word rather than a being and a concept rather than a feeling and god is just energy and religion is just being and religion is just the ritual of feeling and feeling is living but living is not real because reality exists only in dreams and we don't live in dreams because we don't die we just wake up and live again and then is life just a dream and dreams a figment

of a brain's imagination of which is just constructed by the same thing that makes a wooden table as well as the thing that makes stars and we can never actually see a star or be a star for they are just pinholes in the sky that we can never breathe or see or feel or love or die to die to love to feel. Your brain has exploded into colours. As has the world and nothing is no longer static and static is no longer no more understandable than the understanding of everything which is simply no more. Then what do you want? I want nothing. You can't want nothing you must want something that you want so that you can be so that you can need something because we all need something otherwise what is the point of everything?

Nothing.

Billy Parker is a playwright, poet and painter who lives and works in London.

ANONYMOUS

NOTHING LIKE THIS

Just like any other Thursday, there is time for my programme before she gets in from school. I turn the volume to 18 so I can hear it from the kitchen where I am ironing and watching the onions. I never need the pictures. These shows are all the same. There's the doomed teenager whose murder shocks the town and the local sheriff who insists that 'nothing like this ever happens here.'

I take the folded clothes upstairs and put them on Sally's chair. I stand for a minute taking in that sweaty-sweet scent of adolescence that is distinctly her. The skirt I said she couldn't borrow is in a ball on the floor. Her bed is unmade, and it looks like there is a cigarette burn in the curtain. There is a half-eaten bowl of cereal on her desk, brown mosaics cementing the spoon in place.

By the time I get back downstairs the show has got to the bit where the teenager's friends hold a candlelight vigil.

I make a little space on the counter to slice the rolls.

A teacher of the murdered American girl is saying she was full of potential.

Then the mobile rings, and I see it's the school.

Suddenly, I am the mother in Summertown with the beloved dead daughter—and I am being interviewed by a sympathetic journalist and you can tell I've had my hair done—and they intercut my teary-eyed close-up with clips of me being helped into the church—and I am saying 'she wasn't just my daughter she was my best friend.'

Then the front door slams, and I hear her stomping up the stairs as if she wants to cause them pain.

I just let the phone ring and ring.

SIOBHAN LANCASTER

TEN POUND POMS
extract from novel

Stella leaned over and peered out of the porthole plane window at a vista of flaxen flatness spread out before her. Seemingly endless in its vastness, she mused that it was definitely not the 'green and pleasant land' she had hitherto known and was rather fond of, despite the drizzly English weather on many days of the year.

"What fresh hell is this?" her mother seated next to her whispered, as the plane banked and began to descend. What planet had she been transported to?

A sudden thud of wheels on the runway, followed by a strong force of negative speed, thrust the passengers forward in their seats and woke the sleeping from their twenty-four-hour journey in the long metal tube. Stella had briefly wondered upon take-off, how such a massive body of metal could stay afloat in the air, suspended by what? Nothing but air, apparently, but given the aircraft's heavy weight, she had her doubts, making sure to keep her seatbelt fastened for the entire trip, except toilet breaks during which she very much hoped that the plane would not choose to have engine failure.

Plane wheels screeching to a grinding halt were followed by a flurry of activity around Stella: people unfolding their limbs, stretched and smoothed their clothes, hair and rumpled faces. Hurried gathering of belongings in the cabin, from under seats and overhead lockers ensued. A queue gathered in the aisle, into which Stella, her parents and two older brothers managed to slip. Slowly, the line began to move, as passengers shuffled along in exhausted robotic fashion, clutching their squashed possessions. Stella held tight to her teddy bear but dropped some of her crayons on the floor, which were quickly ground into the carpet by the feet of those walking behind her, much to the chagrin of the disapproving air hostess looking on.

"Goodbye," the smiling and immaculate crew exclaimed, as their cattle-like human cargo stepped wearily through the open disembarkation doors. How did they manage to look so good after twenty-four hours, mused many of the crumpled passengers, muttering tiredly back "thanks love" or just "yeah, cheers", before staggering down the steps to the tarmac?

Stepping out of the exit door, Stella felt a wall of heat strike her body with a force that pushed her backwards into her mother's waist directly behind. Holding hands, mother and daughter set about the wobbly descent down the steps and onto the boiling tarmac. Waves of shimmering hotness like a desert mirage, wafted up around their two diminutive forms. By the time the passengers had all trekked across the sticky sun-drenched tar to where the tin shed terminal sat, Stella's face and back dripped with beads of sweat, and the physical effects of a long journey across the world began, in a surge of sickly nausea.

Finally, the hapless group gathered within the galvanised walls of the airless, suffocating terminal structure. A drawling voice rang out, "welcome to Austraya and sunny Adelaide! Ya picked a bonza day to arrive. It's summer and only 84 degrees. Gets even hotter than that, if ya lucky!" The crowd stared incredulously at the smiling, very shiny, dark tan-faced greeter.

Stella looked up at her mother slowly mopping her sweating brow and chest with a tiny hanky, an expression of heavy weariness on her face. Her mother looked down at Stella, with red teary eyes and muttered "oh God, what have we done?"

Siobhan spent many years going walkabout from Ireland to the UK to Australia to the United States to England and is now living in Wales. After a few lives spent working in politics, the law and academia, she is now disabled, so there is nothing else for it but to write about those past lives, real or imagined.

NERYS BEATTIE

THE LITTLE SHOP MOUSE

When the doors have shut, and all is still
The sign says "closed", there's no sound from the till,
A little mouse stirs and wakes from his sleep,
Twitches his nose, then takes a peep
To check that nobody's left inside,
Then yawns and stretches, eyes open wide.
"It's time to play!" he laughs to himself
Then nimbly jumps from his home on the shelf.

Scampering along, he can't wait to see
His cuddly friends and their huge family.
Mattie the Monkey, Wally the Whale
Riley the Rabbit with the soft fluffy tail.
Bashful the Lion and Tad the Tree Frog,
Odell the Octopus, Puffles the Dog.
All of them chatter and dance and play
When all have gone home at the end of the day.

Spinning tops and wooden planes,
Yo-yos, cars and wind-up trains,
Race along the toy room floor—
Who'll be first to the shop's front door?
Mermaids sit and comb their hair,
Unicorns prance, kites fly through the air!
Colourful crayons squiggle and draw
To the sounds of the music box and the dinosaur's roar.

Little mouse nibbles the crumbs from the sweets
And loves to sniff all the beautiful treats.
Candles and perfumes and chocolates galore,
Bubble bath, lotions and potions and more!

He tiptoes up the winding stairs
To look at the paintings, the books and the hares.
He teases a statue and pinches her nose
And wiggles his tail so it brushes her toes.
She smiles and stares but never giggles
And stands perfectly still, despite all the tickles.

Way up high on the wall, there's the sea.
There are hills and mountains, as green as can be!
Rabbits and birds and otters on gold
All the wonderful colours a sight to behold.
He wonders who lives in that pretty, white house
With the garden of flowers. Is it a mouse?

Onwards to the kitchen room,
There are plates and cups and a very small broom.
There's cheese that taunts and grapes he can't eat
Still, it's fun to chase 'round the big table's feet.
When pretty, pink bunting is hung in a line
Little Mouse knows that it's summertime.
He scampers along it and whistles a tune
And with a hop and a skip he's in the next room.

There's silk and velvet, linen and cotton
And such beautiful dresses! He's never forgotten.
Sometimes the Rag Doll admires the clothes
She tries on the hats, but they fall down to her toes!
"Everything here's way too big, what a pity!
I'd love a new hat"—so Mouse tells her she's pretty.
"You don't need a hat; it would cover your hair!"
And he gives her a cuddle and whispers, "there, there".

Sometimes the Toy Room's the weirdest of places
With monsters and witches and strange, scary faces.
"BANG BOOM, BOOM BANG!" The Toy Room's berserk!
But soon they all laugh "it's a firework."
This is the time when winter is here
But nobody's sad, it's the best time of year!

When everything glitters and sparkles inside
Little Mouse and the toys know that soon it's Yule Tide.
The stars and the fairy lights twinkle each night
And high in the sky the moon's wintery white.
Stories of Santa and magical things
Sparkly baubles and angels with wings.
Candy canes, fairies and magical elves
All dance late at night with the toys on the shelves.

Little Mouse feels sad on Christmas Eve
So many toy friends have had to leave.
Santa has been with his present list
And has swept them away, they're terribly missed.
Rag Doll has gone to sit under a tree
Bashful, Wally and Mattie Monkey.
All of them gone to a loving new home
And poor Little Mouse is sitting alone.

When the clock in the tower in the centre of town
Chimes the 5th hour, the sun's just gone down.
Little Mouse snuggles up warm in his bed
Round his neck is a scarf, bobble hat on his head.
All is quiet in the shop at last
But after a week or so has past
The great bell sounds the midnight hour
Twelve big 'DONGS' from the tall clock tower.
A brand-new day and a brand new year
And Little Mouse knows, soon new friends will be here.

Great big boxes, they come through the door
They're filled high with teddies and dollies and more.
"Come in! You're welcome! Hello! Who are you?"
Little Mouse bustles with so much to do.

So next time you're there, and you're looking around
Why don't you see if the mouse can be found?
He lives on a shelf, has a comfortable bed
And sometimes he wears a hat on his head.
His house is somewhere in the Toy Room.
I hope that you'll go and look for him soon.

After many years of travelling and living in London, Nerys has now returned to Pembrokeshire where she lives with her family and small pack of dogs. She started her own business in lockdown, creating jewellery and gifts from recycled copper and other materials, but writing has always been her first passion. Her first children's book *Little Bee's Sneeze* was published in 2019.

BOB REEVES

SEA WITCH

There's a witch in the sea at Caldey,
And the green tressed weeds are her hair,
Her voice is the cry
Of the gull in the sky
And a ten fathom cavern her lair.

She sits weaving the spells
That control ocean swells
And she sings to the crabs and the fish,
Seven seals are her slaves
And bring foam from the waves
Which she eats from an oyster shell dish.

Her magic's the magic of mermaids and pearls,
Of shipwrecks and pirates and whales,
She charms from the sky
With her hurricane eye
The winds that make westerly gales.

So whenever you paddle at Tenby,
Heed well what the gulls have to say ,
Ere that wicked Welsh witch
With her eyes black as pitch
Send sea horses to drag you away.

SONG OF THE WEST WIND

Low tide and summer,
And over the whale humped
Rocks and the reef, sea widow
Weeded, and the crab hissed
And cockle spitting sands.
It came singing and full
Of the pulsing magic of
The bottomless Atlantic.
And it sang where I sat
In the whispering marrammed dunes
And under its siren song
Time ceased and I was
Awake and asleep and
Open and tasting and
My skin flinched and tingles
With a thousand delicious
Electric shocks as the wind
Caressed me, sensual
And with fingers that
Turned and shimmered
The silver underbellies of
The highest trembling leaves
And made harps of the tree tops.
And I was light and sun and water,
And as full of dancing gold
As the ribbed and rippled
Freshwater sands when the
First, flat, inch ankle
Deep and paddling, skimming
Wavelets, glimmering and July sunlit,
Lick and tease and race
Before the jaws of the running surf.
I breathed deep and was fish
And ran with the mackerel,
Through the green and writhing

Kelped and congering depths.
Before the seven seals of Caldey,
And I was bird and flew and
Dived with the great beaked,
Yellow eyed and arrowing gannets.
And I was cloud and gloated
Above the cliffs and over
The patched hills and the
Copsed and meadowed country,
Where the wind made waves in
The grey green sea of the uncut,
Courting, giggling, slapping, sighin hay.
Oh I was all of these and
Lulled and seduced and enchanted
By the breath of the sea
And the voice of the sea.
In the song of the west wind,
I slept.

Bob Reeves was born, lives and works in beautiful Pembrokeshire—the far Western tip of Wales. As a painter and poet he cannot fail to be inspired by the place. His response is immediate and personal . He is part of the circle of this Earth. "Its cycle of tides and seasons continue to entrance me. I seek no escape."

CURTAIN

ACKNOWLEDGEMENTS

Celine's Salon's tour would not have happened if it hadn't been for the kindness and generosity of Robert Hamer, Carl Hopkins and Frances Kingsnorth. I am eternally grateful!

Thank you to:

Grace Cargill and Billy Parker, for being wonderful assistants and volunteers.

Siobhan Lancaster and Nerys Beattie for poster flying and being a massive help in every way!

Robert and Liz Lewis for your art contribution and encouragement.

Murray John and his wife for the use of their wonderful Tenby home—it was hard to leave!

Carolyn Cox and Patrick Ovenden at The Tenby Observer for the review.

Garry Salter for design and production. John O'Neill and Darren Harkin for film, sound and streaming. And Clancy Gebler Davies for support and encouragement.

Bluebell Arts Derry and Frank Rafferty for our collaboration.

Millennium Forum Theatre Derry

Rachael Johnson for hosting myself and our performers at her home—we are truly grateful.

Dawn Izatt and her team at venue Time, Event Space Glasgow.

Mark Lewis, his wife and the trustees of Tenby Museum— can't wait to come back!

Thanks to Dan and all the staff at We Are Cuts.

Lucy Tertia George at Wordville Press for all of her support and believing in me and Celine's Salon. Thank you for Volume 2!

To all of our artists, supporters, friends and family who have been and will continue to be a part of this anthological marvellous journey.

And finally, to Mo Hatt for being so supportive through thick and thin. Big love daddypops!

Celine.

CPSIA information can be obtained
at www.ICGtesting.com
Printed in the USA
LVHW040040270922
729329LV00012B/489